MEG'S CAR

for Thomas

It was a lovely day
for a picnic

Meg Mog and Owl
wanted to go
in a car

So Meg made a spell

Boot and bonnet
Rattle and clang
Make me a car
That goes with a bang

They
all
piled
into
the
new
car

Mog
started
the
engine

The car shot backwards

then
lurched
forward

VROOM
VROOM

It went with a bolt and a jolt

a thump, a bump and a jump

The car started

off,
took
It

and landed

CRAS

in a
tree

So they went to the picnic
on the broomstick

Goodbye!